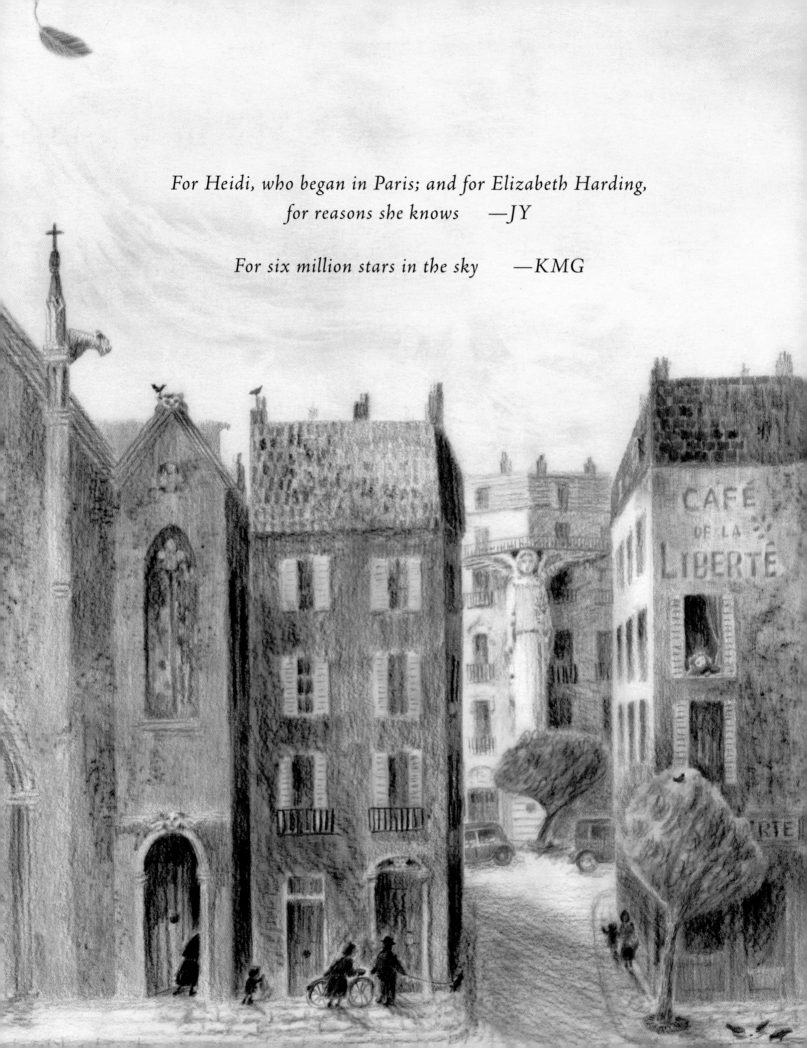

For Heidi, who began in Paris; and for Elizabeth Harding,
for reasons she knows   —JY

For six million stars in the sky   —KMG

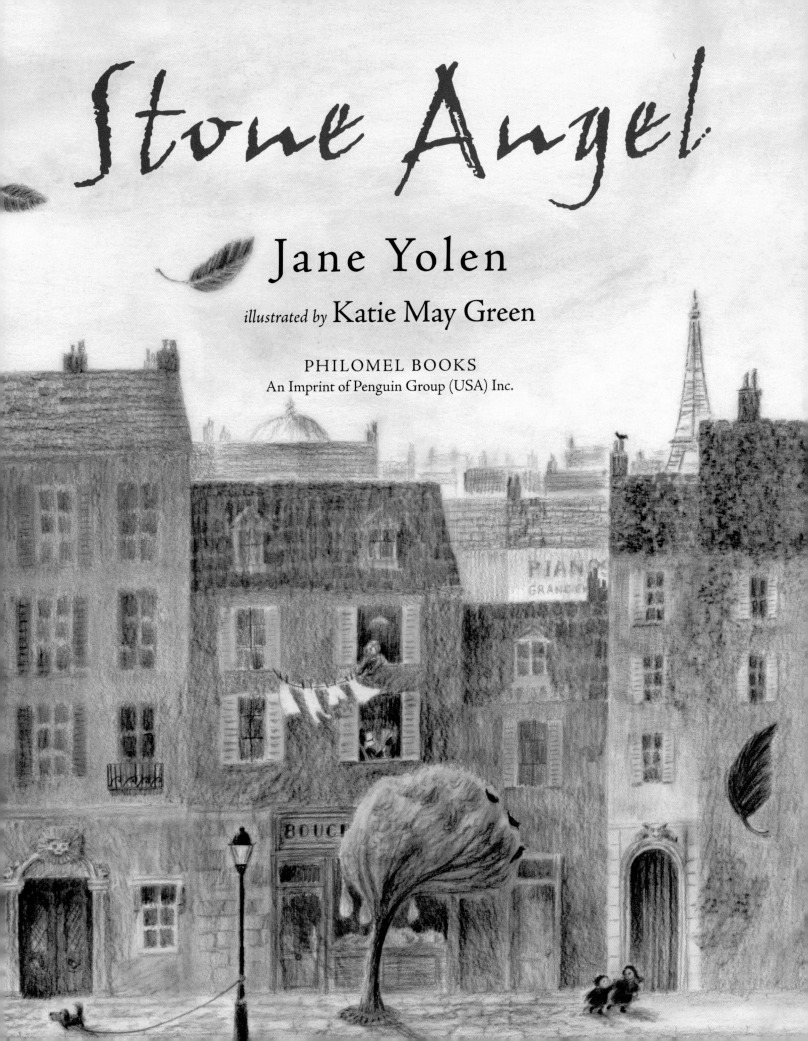

Stone Angel

Jane Yolen

illustrated by Katie May Green

PHILOMEL BOOKS
An Imprint of Penguin Group (USA) Inc.

We ran,
my little brother Aron and I,
down the steps of our house,
along the streets of Paris,
where stone angels and gargoyles
looked down on us
from churches, cathedrals, and homes.

As we ran, the Paris wind—
soft as Maman's hand brushing my hair—
teased little wisps from my braids.
Aron and I skipped along and sang:
"*Au clair de la lune, mon ami Pierrot.*"
Then Aron got a *croissant* from the *pâtisserie*
and gave me a bite.

Every day was the same,
though sometimes I was the one
who had the croissant and he had a *brioche*.
We always waited at the corner for Maman
to lead us across the street, saying,
"You are *mes beaux bébés*,"
though neither of us were babies anymore.

And then one day the bad men came
in their brown shirts, guns in hands.
They made us wear yellow stars on our coats
so everyone would know we were *Juifs*, Jews,
and call us bad names and take away
our houses.
Even Madame Calais at the pâtisserie
turned her back and would not sell us
croissants.
Papa was forced to leave his job
at the observatory,
where he had studied the stars,
and we had to move in with friends
who soon enough had to ask us to leave.
Maman wept and said, "They are not
bad people, just frightened people."
But even as she said this, she held little Aron close.
I pointed to the yellow star on her coat.
"Where there are stars, Maman,
there are angels."
Papa gathered me in his arms, saying,
"There are no angels here."

So we ran.
We ran to the bus stop and took a bus
that drove us away from Paris into the woods.
Once we had picnicked there, but now we went to hide.
We ran deep and deeper into the forest.
"We will be safe here," Papa said,
"till the brown shirts are all gone."
"But what is safe?" Maman asked. What indeed?
There was to be no more school for me,
no more radio, no more soft bed or warm croissants.
Not even a brioche.
We carried blankets, food that would not spoil,
and extra clothes in case we got cold.
Papa brought along a lantern and a knife
and, of course, his star charts.
Maman carried a box of photographs,
a hairbrush, and comb.
Aron hugged his favorite toy soldier.
I had my stuffed bear.

We lived in caves, and lean-tos,
and once in a long-abandoned woodshed,
but none of those were at all like home.
The wind grew cold and bitter.
After a while, we only had the food
we could find in the forest, late berries,
fish in the river, and wild onions,
which made Aron wrinkle his nose at the taste.
"Soon," Maman said, "it will be winter,
but we will eat what we find in nature's cupboard.
We will make the best of it."
She sang us lullabies so we could sleep,
even Papa, before ever laying down herself.
I remembered the tales of children in the forest
watched over by angels, and was not afraid.

People joined us in the woods,
men and women without children.
Partisans, Papa called them.
We knew they were Jews like us.
On their coats were the shadows of stars,
though the stars had been torn off some
time ago.

Maman let us tear off our stars as well,
but I kept mine in my pocket
so the angels would know me.
The women shared food they had brought,
pulling out crusty *baguettes* and cheese rounds,
soft apples with brown spots, and chocolate bars
from great sacks they carried on their backs.
We feasted but did not set any cook fires,
afraid they would show the brown shirts
where we could be found.

Aron and I learned to be quiet,
to become shadows, how to turn invisible,
sleeping all day long, waking only at night.
One of the partisans said we were
still as fawns in a thicket
waiting for their maman to return.
When he said that, his smile was small and swift,
as if he had not practiced smiling for a very long time.
Sometimes we heard marching feet making thunder
or the sound of automobiles grinding along
far-off paths
and shrank even deeper into the darkness
and covered ourselves with leaves.
Aron thought it was a game,
but I knew it was not.
Papa had read me the stories.
Wolves in the forest can walk on two legs.

One day Papa went off with ten of the men.

"A minyan," he said, laughing, though it was no joke.

Instead of prayers, they had guns and hammers and knives.

Their faces were like chiseled rock.

They did not say good-bye, as if saying it made it so.

We waited for two days
till Papa and three of the men returned—
only three—with dark stains on their coats
where the star shadows had been.
The other men never came back.
All the women wept long into the night,
small, snuffling sounds, like animals.
But I did not cry.
I knew they had flown off to be with the angels.

Papa said the forest was too full of dangers,
that now we must go
over the great mountains to Spain,
where we would find a place of boats.
There we would sail away to an island called England,
where our cousin Jacob lived.
I asked if he was young.
"*Non, ma chère,*" said Papa. "Old, like me."
Aron clapped his hands. "Will he have croissants?"
"He has crumpets," Papa said,
which made Aron and me giggle.
Maman sighed. "Is it far?"
"Very far," Papa told her.
"Not as far as a star," I added.
Then Maman laughed, her hand over
her mouth
so the laugh did not go
any farther than the circle of our family.
It did not even go as far as her eyes.

The very next night, after shaking hands with the men
and being kissed on both cheeks by the women
who filled our backpacks with food, we left.
Papa knew how to read the mountains as if they were a map,
but I stared up in the skies looking for angels.
Often the tall mountains hid the stars,
and the angels seemed farther and farther away.
Most times we walked slowly.
Sometimes we ran.
We went up a mountain and down.
And another.
And another.
And another.

Aron caught a fever
and whimpered all the time.
Maman held him close,
sometimes rubbing mountain snow
on his face and hands to cool him down.
After a bit, he got well again,
but he remained very thin and very white.
He had to be carried everywhere.
Even I took a turn.
Mostly Maman kept him tied to her body
in front with a bright red scarf.

"Ask your angels to look after him,"
Maman said,
and I did.

At last, one night, we came down the final mountain
and into a Spanish city with a port filled with small boats.
We found one going across to England.
Papa exchanged his fur hat, Maman her wedding ring,
for our passage over the water
and a telegram to be sent to Cousin Jacob.
I offered my stuffed bear.
"Keep it, little one," the skipper said in very bad French.
"You may need it for comfort, for luck."

I hugged the bear tight.
It was a silent boat, except for the creaking ropes in the wind,
except for the waves slapping against the keel.
We were almost invisible on the moonless tide,
one large shadow on a sea of shadows.
Mothers put their fingers in their babies' mouths
to keep them from crying.
But Aron and I already knew the language of silence.
We had spoken it for so many weeks.

When we reached the far shore, we ran.
We ran down the gangplank
to where Cousin Jacob waited for us,
carrying a sign on which he had printed our family name.
Strong as an angel, he swung Aron up and down.
He took us to his house. *His* house. Not ours.

We lived there for four years, learning English,
eating scones and crumpets that Jacob made.
We went to the English school till the war was over.

When we heard on the radio
that all the men in brown shirts
had gone back to wherever they had come from,
Germany or Austria—"Or Mars," Jacob said—
we all ran out to the main street of the town,
waving flags and singing "God Save the Queen."

Maman said, "Now we can go home. To Paris."
Home, I thought, though it had not seemed like home
when we'd been forced to leave it.

When we sailed back to France,
the boat was filled with laughing people
who sang French songs loudly.
I led them in singing:
"Au clair de la lune, mon ami Pierrot."

Aron remembered little of it.
Everyone clapped and gave me kisses,
first on one cheek, then the other,
calling me an *ange*, an angel,
even though I had no wings.

When we got to Paris, Aron and I ran.
We ran down the street, along the Rue de Turbigo,
where Papa had found an apartment for us.
He had gotten his old job back at the observatory.
Along the way we found a pâtisserie
and bought a croissant for me, a brioche for Aron.
Then we walked farther on, exchanging bites.
Where Rue de Turbigo bent gently, I suddenly looked up.
There—*there*—at number 57, where we were to live,
wearing a long pleated stone gown, wings spread wide,
a sprig of summer in his hand, stood the angel,
the one who had kept us safe in the forest,
in the mountain, over the water, in the cozy English house,
who was now smiling softly to welcome us home.

A Note from the Author

Yes, there was a time when men in brown shirts (Nazis) took over Paris as well as the rest of Europe. A time when Jewish people were thrown out of their jobs as teachers, doctors, professors, shop owners, and hundreds of other jobs. When they were forced to wear identifying yellow stars on their clothes. When Jews and other people (the handicapped, Seventh-Day Adventists, gays, Gypsies, people of color, and more) were routinely killed or rounded up and put into work camps or death camps. This went on for well over five years. It was called World War II.

Yes, the Nazis were finally beaten by the Allies, a coalition of Americans, English, French, Russians, Canadians, and others, though many millions were killed in the fighting, and over ten million more were murdered in the death camps—six million of them Jews—in a horror known as the Holocaust.

Yes, many freedom fighters in Europe—called partisans—took to the woods, where they hid out and fought a guerilla war against the Nazi troops. They also spied, passing on information to the Allies about the death camps and troop movements; rescued downed Allied fliers; and led people across the Pyrenees or the Alps mountains to safety.

And yes, at 57 Rue de Turbigo, where the avenue bends, stands a colossal nine-meter-tall statue of a welcoming angel attached to the wall of an apartment house. The angel's huge feathers brush against the windows of the fourth-floor apartment. The angel is called The Lighthouse Angel—a second-year architecture student had created the angel's original design for a lighthouse competition. (It didn't win!) If you visit Paris, you can see it.

PHILOMEL BOOKS
Published by the Penguin Group | Penguin Group (USA) LLC
375 Hudson Street, New York, NY 10014

USA | Canada | UK | Ireland | Australia | New Zealand | India | South Africa | China
penguin.com | A Penguin Random House Company

Library of Congress Cataloging-in-Publication Data
Yolen, Jane.
The stone angel / Jane Yolen ; illustrated by Katie May Green.   pages cm   Summary: While trying to escape with her family from the Nazis, a young
Jewish French girl feels protected by angels. 1. Holocaust, Jewish (1939–1945)—France—Juvenile fiction. [1. Holocaust, Jewish (1939–1945)—
France—Fiction. 2. Jews—France—Fiction. 3. France—History—German occupation, 1940–1945—Fiction. 4. Escapes—Fiction. 5. Angels—Fiction.]
I. Green, Katie May, illustrator. II. Title. PZ7.Y78Ss 2015 [E]—dc23 2013022476
Manufactured in China by South China Printing Co. Ltd.
ISBN 978-0-399-16741-6
1 3 5 7 9 10 8 6 4 2

Edited by Jill Santopolo. | Design by Semadar Megged. | Text set in 16-point Adobe Jenson Pro.
The illustrations were rendered in mixed media.